Emma Thomson's

felicity Wishes ®

friends forever

and other stories

· How to make your felicity Wishes ·

W I S H

With this book comes an extra special wish for you and your best friend.

Hold the book together at each end and both close your eyes.

Wriggle your noses and think of a number under ten.

Open your eyes, whisper the numbers you thought of to each other.

Add these numbers together. This is your

✩ Magic Number ✩

you

best friend

Place your little finger on the stars, and say your magic number out loud together. Now make your wish quietly to yourselves. And maybe, one day, your wish might just come true.   Love

felicity
x

For Mathilde Roque de Pinho
with extra special wishes
E.V.T

Emma Thomson's
felicity Wishes®

FELICITY WISHES
Felicity Wishes © 2000 Emma Thomson
Licensed by White Lion Publishing

Text and Illustrations © 2005 Emma Thomson

First published in Great Britain in 2005 by Hodder Children's Books

A Catalogue record for this book is available from the British Library

ISBN 0 340 90241 8

Printed and bound in China by Imago

The paper and board used in this paperback by Hodder Children's Books are natural recyclable
products made from wood grown in sustainable forests. The manufacturing processes
conform to the environmental regulations of the country of origin.

Hodder Children's Books
A division of Hodder Headline Ltd, 338 Euston Road, London NW1 3BH

CONTENTS

Friends Forever

PAGE 7

Safe Secrets

PAGE 29

Singing Success

PAGE 53

Friends Forever

"What is that noise?!!" shouted Felicity
Wishes above the din.

"It sounds like someone's having
their tooth pulled out," said Polly, who
knew about these sorts of things. She
was going to be a tooth fairy when
she left the School of Nine Wishes.

"It's coming from the changing
rooms," said Holly, clamping her
hands over her ears. "Let's investigate!"

The three fairy friends dashed off in the direction of the games block. The closer they got, the worse the noise sounded.

"SooooooooLlllllllllaaaaaaaaFffffffaa aaaaa."

"Are you all right in there?" shouted Felicity, banging on the door.

"MMMeeeeerrrraaaayyyy? Coooooouldn't be more better!" wailed a familiar voice.

"Daisy?!" exclaimed Felicity, Holly and Polly together.

"Yes," said Daisy smiling as she peeped her head around the door.

"What were you doing in there?" asked Polly, curious.

"I'm auditioning for the school choir after lunch so I was just warming up my voice."

"You were singing?!" said Felicity, trying to hide her shock.

"It sounded like you were in pain,"

mumbled Holly under her breath.

"I always sing to my plants and they seem to enjoy it so I thought I would give the choir a go," said Daisy, oblivious to the fairies stunned faces.

Friendship to Felicity was everything and she tried with all her heart to be the best friend she could to everyone, especially Holly, Polly and Daisy. Sometimes, though, it was hard – there was no friendly way of telling Daisy that she couldn't sing a single note in tune.

"Maybe we could do a group audition so we can all join the choir?" said Felicity, thinking on her toes. "After all, best friends always do the best things together."

"What a great idea!" said Daisy, excited. "We will stand out much more as a group."

"Yeah, that's a great idea," said Holly sarcastically, who had been planning to shine with a solo performance.

"Well, we've only got half an hour left to practise so we had better get started," said Polly.

* * *

At last it was the fairy friends turn to sing. Holding each other's hands, they nervously walked up on stage and sang their favourite song – Friends Forever.

Felicity had encouraged Holly and Polly to sing as loudly as possible so

that Daisy's voice almost sounded in key.

"Well done, fairies," said Miss Quaver, clapping when their performance ended. "If you two would like to go and wait at the back of the hall," she said pointing to Daisy and Polly, "and you two can wait over there," she said motioning to Felicity and Holly.

"NEXT!" she boomed, looking down at her long list.

"I wonder why we've been separated," whispered Holly to Felicity as they joined a small group of fairies by the piano.

"I hope Daisy and Polly have made it into the choir," Felicity whispered back. She was worrying that Miss Quaver had split them into groups of 'winners' and 'losers'.

"It's us, not them, who haven't got in," interrupted a very tall fairy in a very sparkly blue dress.

"I only auditioned for fun," she continued. "My voice is so squeaky that I never expected to be chosen for a moment."

Holly looked shocked. She wasn't used to losing anything, especially when it came to singing competitions. She strongly believed that she was a star in the making, and being turned down by the school choir wasn't even worth thinking about.

"Well, if that's the case," whispered Felicity to Holly, "I shall be very happy. A true friend always wants the best for their friends, and Daisy really wanted to be in the choir more than any of us."

"Told you!" said the tall fairy, pointing towards the back of the hall.

All the fairies that had been sent there, including Daisy and Polly, were whooping with glee as Miss Quaver tried to calm them down.

"Fairies! Please simmer down, at least until I've had a chance to talk to the other group."

As Miss Quaver made her way over to the piano, Felicity breathed a sigh of relief for Daisy, but Holly was frozen on the spot – her reputation would be in ruins if she didn't get into the choir.

"All of you have very high voices," began Miss Quaver.

"See!" whispered the tall fairy to Felicity as she got ready to leave.

"It takes a wide range of voices to make a successful choir. Some that are lower like trebles and tenors," and Miss Quaver motioned to the fairies at the back of the hall, "and some that are higher like yourselves."

Holly gulped. Things didn't look good.

"Congratulations fairies," Miss Quaver continued, "you've been selected to be the descant, soprano and altos in the School of Nine Wishes Fairy Choir."

"We did it!" said Felicity hugging Holly in a frenzy of flapping wings. "We all did it!" she shouted, running towards Daisy and Polly for a group hug.

* * *

But over the next few weeks, Felicity discovered that being in the choir wasn't as much fun as she had first imagined.

There were all sorts of things to learn – sight-reading music, breathing properly using your tummy and learning Miss Quaver's hand movements for when to 'come in', 'sing softly', 'sing loudly', or sometimes 'not sing at all!'

But the hardest part for Felicity though wasn't all the new things she had to learn, it was something for which she felt partly responsible...

"There's no nice way of putting it," Felicity overheard a fellow choir fairy saying to her friend, "Daisy just can't sing."

"I know," agreed the friend, "it's making us all sound bad."

Felicity later discovered that most fairies in the Treble and Tenor group had

been saying this amongst themselves for quite some time. So she set about making it better.

"I've been thinking," she said to Daisy, Holly and Polly one breaktime. "I think we should all give up the choir."

"Give up?" they chorused, shocked.

"Yes," said Felicity earnestly. "Since we've been put in groups, we hardly ever get to spend any time together."

"Well," said Polly thoughtfully, "if we're true friends we'd make time, so why don't we all make sure we get together for at least one breaktime a day."

Holly and Daisy quickly agreed.

Felicity wasn't expecting it to be so hard to convince them to leave.

"Um, it's not only that, there's something else that's making me unhappy about staying in the choir," she said trying hard to think of something quick.

"What?" urged Daisy.

Holly and Polly knew Felicity was up to something but couldn't quite put their finger on what it was.

"Um…" said Felicity floundered.

Suddenly she had a much better plan. "I'm worried that my singing isn't as good as everyone else's and I'm letting everyone down," she burst out, hoping that a little white lie wouldn't hurt too much.

After lots of protests and discussions, Felicity explained that the only way she would feel confident to stay in the choir would be with support from her friends. When Daisy, Polly and Holly all offered to give her extra lessons, she didn't refuse. With luck her plan would work.

"Thanks for doing this," said Felicity, when she arrived at Daisy's house the next night.

"Oh, that's quite all right," said Daisy. "If you believe you can do anything, you can!" she said, leading Felicity through to her sitting room where Holly and Polly were warming up their voices.

"Right," she said handing Felicity a hairbrush, "I find a microphone always helps. From the top. One, two, three..."

Felicity was silent.

"Go on!" said Daisy. "Surely you're not shy in front of your best friends?"

"Why don't we do it together,"

suggested Felicity. "I'll do my high soprano part, and you do your low tenor part, and Holly and Polly can be the voice coaches. Then we can see where I'm going wrong."

"OK, let's start from the top again," agreed Daisy.

As soon as Felicity and Daisy started to sing, Holly and Polly found it almost impossible to stifle their giggles – Felicity was great but Daisy was truly awful.

After two hours of constant singing, Felicity and Daisy collapsed on the sofa, exhausted, and Holly and Polly gave a huge sigh of relief – they didn't think their tummies could take any more giggling.

"Don't be angry with us," said Holly and Polly, sinking further into the sofa, still giggling.

"Why ever should we be angry with you?" asked Felicity confused.

Holly pulled out a tape recorder from behind the sofa.

"We secretly recorded you," said Polly nervously.

"What a good idea!" said Daisy. "Felicity, now you will soon see that you had no reason to leave the choir."

Daisy pressed the rewind button on the machine. Felicity looked awkward.

"There's no need to listen," she said looking helplessly at Holly and Polly. "Really, I already know I'm dreadful."

"There's no such thing as dreadful," said Daisy. "Practice makes perfect and I think you'll find you don't need much practice at all." She set the tape recorder on the table, pressed play and sat back.

As soon as the singing started, a look of horror fell across Daisy's face.

"I must have it on the wrong speed!" she said quickly sitting forward and studying the machine. "You didn't sound this bad," she said to Felicity patting her hand.

The more the machine played the worse the singing sounded, and slowly Daisy began to realise that the awful din they were hearing, wasn't Felicity's singing, but her own.

"Oh Felicity!" Daisy sobbed uncontrollably. "I'm awful! How could I not have known. You sounded perfect, and I was SO out of tune!"

"You weren't that bad," said Holly and Polly comfortingly.

"Remember what you said when I first arrived?" said Felicity with an arm around Daisy. " 'If you believe you can do anything, you can.' We can do this together, Daisy. That's what friends are for."

"You really think so?" asked Daisy wiping her eyes.

"Really," said Felicity turning over the tape and handing the hairbrush to Daisy.

"Right," she said, "you're the one who said 'practice makes perfect'. So, from the top. One, two, three…" And Holly and Polly pressed record.

* * *

Every night after school Felicity and Daisy practised, and every night the recordings they made got better and better.

Felicity even noticed that there was a lot less whispering in choir practice behind Daisy's back than there used to be.

One evening, as Felicity and Daisy were sitting back listening (without cringing!) to the recording they had just made, there was a knock on the door.

"Miss Quaver!" said Daisy surprised.

"Oh Daisy! I didn't know you lived

here," she said, taken aback. "I was just flying home when I heard a wonderful duet version of the music we're learning in choir. I had to find out who it was."

"Oh, it's a recording," said Daisy showing Miss Quaver into the house.

Miss Quaver joined them until the tape had finished playing.

"Beautiful!" she said almost in a daze. "Singing a duet is much, much harder than singing in a choir."

"Yes," agreed Daisy and Felicity.

"In a choir tiny mistakes can be covered easily, but with two voices it has to be perfect. This is the best duet I've ever heard!" said Miss Quaver dreamily.

Felicity and Daisy's cheeks blushed with delight.

"Do you know where I can get hold of a copy?" asked Miss Quaver.

"You can have this one if you like," said Daisy handing over the tape.

"That's very generous of you. Who is this then?" said Miss Quaver, turning over the tape in her hand. "Let me guess Anatella Bellingo and Dame Charlotta Musica?"

"It's us," said Daisy.

"Oh, I understand this is your tape, dear," said Miss Quaver inspecting it more closely, "but who is it singing?"

"No, it really is us," repeated Felicity proudly and she explained about their extra practice sessions.

* * *

At the end of the next choir rehearsal the next day Miss Quaver had a special announcement to make.

"I am proud to say that the School of Nine Wishes Fairy Choir now performs this piece of music perfectly, and for that you must congratulate yourselves. I am so confident in your ability that I have decided to enter us into an international competition, with one special change – best friends, Felicity and Daisy, will perform the middle section as a duet."

The fairy choir cheered with glee, especially Daisy who for the first time ever, cheered in time with everyone else!

Best friends......

......do the best
things together

Safe Secrets

"It's really not like Miss Quaver to be late," whispered Felicity Wishes to Polly as they sat in the school hall waiting for choir practice to begin.

"I hope she turns up soon," said Daisy, concerned. "We've only got two more weeks before the competition and there are still sections of the music that need work."

Suddenly Fairy Godmother walked in.

"I'm afraid Miss Quaver won't be available this lunchtime," she announced. "I suggest you either practise by yourselves or go outside and enjoy the beautiful weather." And with that she fluttered out.

"Practise by ourselves?!" exclaimed Polly. "How can we? It's impossible!"

Reluctant as Felicity was to admit that anything was impossible, she had to agree with Polly on this one. Even though the choir could all sing in tune now, they couldn't yet sing in time! They would be all over the place without Miss Quaver.

"I'm sure Miss Quaver will be back tomorrow," said Felicity positively to everyone, "and we've still got a whole two weeks to go before the competition. Let's go and enjoy the sunshine!"

* * *

But for the rest of the week, Miss Quaver didn't turn up for lunchtime choir practice, and the fairies were beginning to worry. If they had any chance of winning the competition, they would have to practise night and day for the next week.

"Fancy a super-frothy milkshake at Sparkles?" asked Holly when the last bell rang on Friday afternoon. "We need to decide where to have our picnic tomorrow."

"I'm afraid I can't," said Felicity, not looking as disappointed as she normally did when she had to miss a visit to Sparkles. "I've got to fly to Bloomfield this afternoon."

"That's a shame," said Polly. "What are you going there for?"

Felicity faked a glum expression, "Oh nothing much… just a big surprise for our picnic!" she said grinning wildly.

"Tell us! Tell us!" begged her friends.

"It's a surprise!" she said, picking

up her school bag and flying towards the door. "You'll have to wait until tomorrow!"

* * *

Felicity loved surprises almost as much as her friends and the thought of surprising them made her wings jiggle with excitement.

The cake shop in Bloomfield was one of the best in the whole of fairy world. 'Sticky Bun' in Little Blossoming was great for everyday things like doughnuts, cream cakes and sugar twists but if you wanted something extra-special, 'Sweet Treat Delights' was unrivalled.

"Order number fifty-six!" shouted a fairy assistant from behind the counter. "A double strawberry cream tower with a frosted sparkle finish," she continued to bellow.

"It's mine!" said Felicity licking her lips.

"It'll be five minutes while we wrap
it. How are you getting it home?"

"Flying?" said Felicity, slightly
confused.

The assistant laughed. "I don't think you'll be flying anywhere with this, unless you want to wear it rather than eat it! Take a seat and I'll get the packing fairies to fix you up with a set of wheels."

While Felicity patiently waited, she admired rows upon rows of delicious cakes – gooey chocolate cakes sprinkled with white choc icicles, voluptuous meringues covered in tiny raspberries and towering sponge cakes speckled with mouth-watering fruits.

Out of the corner of her eye, a tiny pink cake covered in sparkling frosted icing caught Felicity's eye – it was so delicate yet looked so yummy too. The tag didn't say what it was called, it just had the number fifty-three printed on it.

"Beautiful, isn't it?" said another

fairy in the queue. "It's a Magical Get Well Gateau – the first cake ever to make poorly fairies better," she explained.

"It looks good enough to be poorly for!" said Felicity.

"I wouldn't say that," said the fairy. "It's actually a very complex recipe with over a hundred magical ingredients. It can only be ordered with a certificate from your doctor and its healing properties are said to be stronger than the wishes of over eighty fairies!"

Felicity was speechless.

"Order number fifty-six, ready to go!" shouted the assistant.

"Here!" said Felicity, holding her ticket in the air and saying goodbye to the fairy in the queue.

The cake was ENORMOUS! It was so tall Felicity couldn't even see over the top of it!

"Goodness Felicity! I hope that's not all for you!" came a familiar voice from behind the cake.

Felicity peered around the cake box.

"Miss Quaver! What are you doing here?"

"Oh, just picking up a cake," said Miss Quaver, looking slightly flustered.

Felicity noticed the tiny pink box Miss Quaver was trying to hide behind her back and also noticed the tag clearly reading 'Fifty-three'.

Felicity gasped.

"Well I have got to dash," said Miss

Quaver running out of the door before Felicity could say anything.

Even though Miss Quaver was Felicity's music teacher, she was also her friend too and Felicity couldn't help but feel that a problem shared was a problem halved. Miss Quaver hadn't been at choir practice all week but it hadn't crossed Felicity's mind that she could be ill. She really wanted to help Miss Quaver but she didn't know how.

* * *

With every careful step of her long way home, Felicity thought about Miss Quaver.

"I suppose accepting that friends sometimes have secrets they don't want to share," Felicity decided, "is also a big part of being a good friend. The best way I can be a good friend to Miss Quaver is to keep her secret safe."

* * *

The next day Holly, Polly, Daisy and Felicity all met up for their picnic. When they saw the amazing frosted double cream tower cake they nearly fainted.

"I can't believe you got it home in one piece!" said Holly, impressed.

"Now I understand why you wanted to have the picnic in your back garden!" said Daisy, trying to work out where to take the first bite.

"They had incredible cakes in the shop," said Felicity with her mouth full. "There was even a Magical Get Well Gateau that makes poorly fairies better."

"Oh, I know all about it!" said Polly, excited. "It was developed years ago by Professor Magikalus. There was an article about it in last week's edition of Fairy Science as she's just brought out a new and improved recipe. The cake is made deep in the Flocktogether Hills and prepared by a team of specially trained cooks."

Felicity was fascinated. "Do you still have the article?"

"Yes, it's got a great toothpaste advert that I want to save for my scrapbook – I'll bring it into school on Monday."

* * *

When Polly gave Felicity the article on Monday she didn't even read it before she popped it into an envelope and placed it on Miss Quaver's desk when no one was looking.

"I can't believe she's not here again!" said one of the altos behind Felicity in the hall.

"I had Miss Quaver for double-music this morning," said Polly to Felicity, "and she rushed out just as we sat down."

Felicity was more certain than ever now that Miss Quaver was unwell.

All the fairies in the School of Nine Wishes Fairy Choir watched the hands of the clock tick by. Suddenly the hall door flew open and everyone sighed with relief, until they saw it wasn't Miss Quaver, but Fairy Godmother.

"Dear fairies," she began, "I'm afraid Miss Quaver can't be with you again today. Maybe tomorrow?" she said, trying to sound optimistic.

For some fairies, this news was too much to bear. Disgruntled moans filled the room as fairies started to panic about the competition.

"But Fairy Godmother, we've got a competition in a week's time. If we don't practise we'll never win and they'll be no point in taking part," Holly burst out.

"From what I understand," said Fairy Godmother addressing them all, "Miss Quaver has gone on an emergency trip to the Flocktogether Hills. I'm certain she'll be back tomorrow and your practice will resume then. Now try not to worry too much – I am sure everything will work out OK in the end." And with that she was gone.

"Well," said a tall fairy standing up on her chair and addressing the rest of the group, "if Miss Quaver can't be bothered to turn up for

practice any more then
neither can I! I'm leaving.
Who's with me?"

Unhappy mumbles
filled the hall.

"You can't leave!" said
Felicity standing up. "None
of you can leave! Think of
all the hard work we've
all put in to this. We can
win this competition, we
really can!"

"Who cares?" said a fairy with plaits
standing next to Felicity. "Miss Quaver
certainly doesn't!"

"Yeah!" There were agreeing nods
from most of the fairies in the room.

"Of course Miss Quaver cares! Think
of all the time she spent teaching us
and all the things we've learned,"
said Felicity frantically.

If only she could tell them that Miss
Quaver wasn't well then they'd all

understand, but Felicity knew being a true friend meant keeping that secret safe.

"Think what you like," said the tall fairy, who sounded more disappointed and hurt than angry. "I'm off, and I'm not coming back!" She got down from her chair, threw down her music and left the hall.

Slowly everyone followed except Felicity, Holly, Polly and Daisy.

Carefully, Daisy began to pick up all the music sheets. "There must be something we can do," she said desperately.

"Without a choir mistress, there is very little we can do," said Holly.

"Leave it with me," said Felicity positively. "Remember friends forever stick together!" she said raising her wand and they all touched wands and smiled.

* * *

Felicity could hardly fly straight when she flew into school the next morning. She had been up most of the night making a gigantic poster to put up on the notice board.

"Wow!" said Holly when she saw it. "I can't believe you actually found a new choir mistress between leaving us last night and now."

IMPORTANT NOTICE

for The School of Nine Wishes Fairy Choir. Substitute Choir Mistress would like all members to attend special after-school competition practice.

"I didn't know that there was another choir mistress in Little Blossoming," said Polly.

Felicity blushed and looked down at her toes.

"Well I haven't actually found anyone yet," she whispered. "If I can't find anyone in time, then I thought I could have a go myself," she said, waving her wand around like a conductor.

Holly, Polly and Daisy looked at each other uneasily.

"Felicity, yesterday lunchtime you stood up for Miss Quaver but in doing so you went from being the most popular fairy in the school to the most unpopular one. I think you're risking the few friends you still have on your side if you think that's a good idea," said Holly.

Polly and Daisy nodded quietly behind Holly, trying not to upset Felicity.

Felicity was hurt to think that being true to the friendship of one person might result in the loss of other friends, but she was undeterred.

"I'd better get looking for a substitute Choir Mistress then!" she said as she flew off, out of the school gates, over the hill, down a lane, and up a tiny windy path that led to Miss Quaver's house.

* * *

If anyone knew where Felicity would find a new choir mistress, it would be Miss Quaver. Felicity only hoped she wasn't too sick for visitors.

Tentatively she rang the bell.

"Hello," said a beautiful fairy as she opened the door.

"I think I may have the wrong house," said Felicity apologetically, "I was looking for Miss Quaver."

"I'm afraid she's out at the moment," said the fairy. "I'm her best friend, Miss Musica. Can I help?"

Felicity felt sure she had heard the name

before and then she suddenly realised.

"Dame Charlotta Musica?!" she gasped. "The world famous opera singer?"

"Yes, I'm surprised you've heard of me. I've been out of the public eye for quite some time now," she giggled shyly.

Felicity wasn't speechless very often but at this moment she couldn't make a sound!

"Between you and me," said Miss Musica, "I've been very poorly but my lovely friend Miss Quaver has nursed me back to health. She even found me a special cake all the way from Flocktogether Hills that made me feel better than ever!"

Felicity was delighted that Miss Musica was feeling better and just as delighted to hear that Miss Quaver wasn't ill.

* * *

The School of Nine Wishes Fairy Choir gathered in the hall after school. They were looking forward to meeting their new choir mistress.

As Felicity walked on stage to rapturous cheers, Holly, Daisy and Polly sank deeper into their seats – Felicity had many talents but she certainly wasn't a choir mistress!

"It gives me great pleasure to announce that Miss Quaver will resume normal choir practice as of tomorrow lunchtime!" said Felicity.

Everyone in the room cheered when they heard the news.

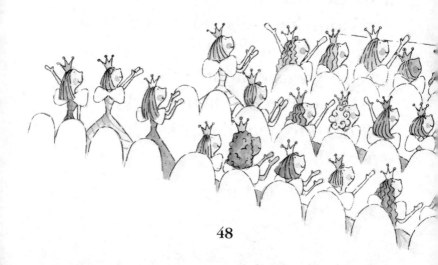

"But for this afternoon only, we have a very special substitute teacher who I'm sure will make up for all the practice sessions we've missed. I am thrilled to introduce the world famous opera singer, and more importantly the best friend of Miss Quaver – Dame Charlotta Musica!"

Holly, Polly, and Daisy nearly fell off their seats when Dame Musica walked onto the stage.

Miss Quaver slipped in through the back door and gave a little wave to Felicity and the other students. She was looking forward to hearing her friend sing too.

"I don't know how you do it!" said Daisy when Felicity finally sat back down in her seat.

"All you have to do is remember that friendship is the best magic there is!" Felicity replied, beaming.

True friends will
be there always

even when it's hard

Singing Success

All the fairies in the School of Nine Wishes Choir had been putting in hours of extra practice for the Fairy International Singing Competition.

Felicity Wishes had been singing so much over the last week that her voice was barely a whisper.

"I hope it comes back in time for the competition!" she croaked to Holly, Polly and Daisy. They were in another choir practice with their teacher, Miss Quaver, who had just allowed them a five-minute break.

"So do I," said Daisy. "It'll be hard for me to do a duet without a partner!"

Felicity tried to giggle but very little came out.

"You must rest your voice," said Polly sensibly. "There are only a few days to go before the competition."

"Don't worry, I'll take your place if your voice hasn't improved," said Holly grinning mischievously.

Felicity hoped with all her heart she'd make a full recovery. She knew Holly would do a good job but didn't want to risk losing her chance to duet with Daisy.

"Really Felicity, you must not speak at all before the competition," said Miss Quaver, the choir mistress, earnestly.

"OK," said Felicity, clamping her hands over her mouth as she realised she'd spoken!

"Remember, not a single word to anybody," Miss Quaver continued sternly. "Hopefully by the time we get to the Arpeggio Mountains your voice will be back and stronger than ever."

Felicity raised her eyebrows at Holly, Polly and Daisy. Not talking was going to be difficult, especially with her best friends.

* * *

Before the fairies knew it, it was time for the choir to set off on the long coach journey to the Arpeggio Mountains. Many of the fairies were travelling further than they'd ever been before.

The familiar sites of their own hometown transformed into magical landscapes that the fairies had only seen in books.

"Isn't it breathtaking?" said Daisy, pressing her nose up against the window.

Felicity nodded enthusiastically.

"I said, isn't it breathtaking?" repeated Daisy, forgetting that Felicity wasn't allowed to speak.

Felicity tapped Daisy on the shoulder and nodded so enthusiastically she thought her crown might fall off!

"Oops, sorry!" said Daisy as she realised her mistake.

* * *

Felicity wasn't her normal perky self during the journey. She was finding it really difficult not to speak to her best friends, especially when they were gossiping about the latest edition of Fairy Girl. She longed to join in the conversation.

"I bet you wish you could speak?" asked Polly, guessing what her best friend had been thinking.

Felicity looked surprised and then nodded. There was no point trying to explain without a voice that her best friend had just read her mind.

"It looks like I just read your mind!" said Polly giving her a hug "Don't worry, your voice will be back soon."

Polly and Felicity had been best friends for what seemed like forever. They were so close that they often said the same things together at the same time.

Sometimes they even tried to telephone each other at exactly the same minute only to find out that the other one was engaged trying to phone them.

"It's funny, isn't it?" said Polly, thinking of something to make her friend smile. "I've got so used to guessing what you're thinking, I bet I can guess what you've packed!"

Felicity drew a question mark in the air.

"Stripy tights!" said Polly giggling. Felicity always wore stripy tights so you didn't have to be a mind reader to guess that she would have packed these.

Suddenly Felicity's face went pale and for once Polly had no idea what she was thinking.

"Are you feeling travel sick?" asked Daisy.

"Do you want me to ask Miss Quaver to stop the coach?" asked Holly concerned.

Felicity shook her head and scribbled a quick note on the back of Fairy Girl.

I've left the suitcase containing the choir outfits at the bus stop!

"Oh goodness," said Polly, realising the enormity of the problem.

"What in fairy world are we all going to wear for our performance?" said Holly, starting to panic.

"It's too late to go back and we're too far away for anyone to reach us," said Daisy.

Felicity was literally speechless!

* * *

Felicity had always been a keen dressmaker. Her attention to detail required patience that no other fairy in the School of Nine Wishes had.

Even before Miss Quaver had

thought about entering the choir into the competition she had asked Felicity to make something special for them to wear. She felt that wearing the same outfit would make the fairies really feel part of the choir together.

Felicity had created something amazing – a beautiful, silver sparkling dress with specially sewn-in wings.

When Miss Quaver saw it she immediately arranged for it to be copied for each and every fairy in the choir – she was sure that with these outfits, the fairies would feel so confident that they'd win the competition easily.

* * *

The next day at breakfast in the hotel

Miss Quaver made an announcement:

"Fairies, I'm afraid I have a bit of bad news. Unfortunately our outfits for the competition have...erm, gone astray," she said, trying not to hurt Felicity's feelings. She knew she was feeling bad enough as it was.

The group of excited fairies fell silent. Without their outfits, they felt they didn't have a chance in the competition.

"Well, at least it's just the dresses and not our voices that are lost," said Holly, speaking louder than she intended.

"You all have wonderful voices and I know we can win this competition on the merit of your voices alone," said Miss Quaver, trying to reassure everyone, especially Felicity. But Felicity still felt dreadful and was determined to make it up to everyone.

* * *

The rest of the morning was spent registering for the competition.

The lobby of the town hall was filled with thousands of fluttering fairy wings.

Even Miss Quaver was surprised at how many schools were arriving.

"Do you think we've got a chance?" Daisy asked her teacher, rather nervously.

"I believe we can do it but the most important thing is that you all do too," Miss Quaver replied confidently.

"But the dresses…" said Daisy sadly, "we've nothing to show that we're a team."

"Your voices will do that," said Miss Quaver. "Some fairies will look good but you will sound fantastic!"

* * *

Holly had always prided herself on being the most fashionable fairy in the School of Nine Wishes but as she looked around the town hall she was

amazed at what some of the other
fairies were wearing.

The fashions here were so much
more adventurous than those at
home. Holly was determined to find
out their top fashion tips and made a
beeline for the group of fashionable
fairies in the corner of the room.

She hadn't been chatting to the
fairies about their stunning outfits for
long, before Felicity spotted her friend
and flew over to join her.

"These are my new friends Pinca,
Suvi, and Pie. Aren't their dresses
amazing?" said Holly to Felicity as
she gently stroked the fine shimmering
rainbow material.

"Hello," said the fairies, all at once and in tiny squeaky voices.

"They're unusual names," said Felicity. "Where are you from?"

"From here!" they all replied at the same time again.

"You must be brilliant at singing," said Holly enviously. "I hear the acoustics in the mountains are wonderful."

"No, not really," said Pie, "but we really need to win the prize." And she twirled around to display the full colours of her glorious skirt.

* * *

Pinca, Suvi and Pie invited Felicity, Holly, Polly and Daisy to visit their school that afternoon. Holly couldn't wait to see what the rest of the Arpeggio Mountain School fairies were wearing! But when they arrived, Holly couldn't believe her eyes. Instead of a shimmering mass of gorgeous clothes, the fairies were wearing drab, threadbare dresses and their school was just as scruffy.

"As you can see," said Pie, "we're from a very basic fairy school. Up here in the mountains it's very difficult to get anything."

"That's why we want to win the competition prize of modern school equipment," explained Suvi.

"But how did you manage to make your beautiful competition dresses?" asked Holly, confused.

"Every fairy in the school contributed

a little towards our outfits," said Pinca. "There are only three of us in the choir so it's important that we look like a proper group."

"It is important, isn't it?" said Felicity sadly thinking of their dresses that had been left behind. "Sharing something similar brings everyone together."

Suddenly a tiny bell rang.

"Get ready!" said Pie, "That was the lunch-time bell."

But before Felicity, Holly, Polly and Daisy could ask her what they should be ready for, they were suddenly mobbed by a hundred inquisitive friendly fairy faces, all wanting to know where they were from!

* * *

All through lunch, Felicity and her friends were asked question after question about where they lived, what they ate, what they liked doing and whether they'd like to stay forever!

The mountain fairies didn't have much food but still managed to put on a fairy feast for Felicity and her friends.

"I've never met so many friendly fairies before," said Felicity to the others as they flew back to the hotel that afternoon.

"I know," said Polly. "They had nothing compared to us, yet they gave us everything."

"The fairies at the Arpeggio Mountain School are a true example of good friendship," said Daisy wistfully. "I hope they win the competition."

"I don't think they will," said Holly in a hushed whisper.

"How do you know?" asked Daisy taken aback.

"I heard them practising and they were awful. Not one note was in tune!"

✳ ✳ ✳

The day of the competition arrived and Felicity, Holly, Polly and Daisy flew as fast as they could to the town hall.

Exciting plans for preparations swept them through the doors in a frenzy of fluttering wings.

Everywhere around them fairies were getting ready for the start of the competition.

Fairies practised scales loudly in corners, added last minute touches to their outfits and frantically dashed in and out of the large swing doors that led to the stage.

With no new outfits to change into there was very little for the School of Nine Wishes Choir fairies to do, except sit and wait for their turn.

Pushing their way through the crowds Pie, Pinca and Suvi headed towards Felicity, carrying a large box.

"Thank goodness we've found you in time," said Pie, handing over the box with a sigh of relief. "You left without these."

Felicity looked down at the box, confused.

"They're a present. We give them to friends who visit the school to remember us by. There should be enough here for everyone in your choir."

Slowly Felicity opened the box to reveal twenty stunning garlands made from the most beautiful flowers in the Arpeggio Mountains.

"Oh Pie!" said Felicity awestruck.

"Thank you! You've given us so much already."

"Wow!" said Holly, catching sight of the beautiful garlands.

"You don't know how perfect these are," said Daisy. "We accidentally left our competition outfits behind and now we'll have something that we can all wear as a team."

* * *

Before the competition began, Pie, Suvi and Pinca each carefully placed one of their homemade garlands on their new friends. They had just finished placing the last when they were called to the stage over the tannoy.

"Good luck," called Felicity as she waved them off with crossed fingers.

"Fairies," said Miss Quaver clapping her hands for attention. "we're next. Remember to breathe deeply. Sing with the friendship that's in all of our hearts and wear your garlands with pride. We can do this!" she said, leading the way to the double doors. "Let's sing to win!"

* * *

The School of Nine Wishes Fairy Choir sang more beautifully then they had ever done before.

Relaxed in their usual clothes and confident with their garlands, every fairy sang every single note perfectly.

Even the judges were in awe when Felicity and Daisy sang their duet.

It had been a tough competition, but their performance was truly exceptional.

No one was surprised when the five judges finally stood up on the stage and revealed that the School of Nine Wishes Fairy Choir had won.

With tears in her eyes, Miss Quaver went to collect the prize.

"Thank you. Thank you," she said. "On behalf of the School of Nine Wishes Choir I'd like to accept this beautiful trophy which we will treasure forever. We are a very special school as we are lucky enough to have lots of lovely things including a strong sense of friendship. As a return gesture of friendship, we would like to give the prize of the school equipment to the Arpeggio Mountain School."

The audience erupted in enormous cheers which turned into cries of:

"More! More! Encore! Encore!"

Standing up with pride, the School of Nine Wishes Choir made their way back to the stage.

"Where's Felicity?" whispered Holly, noticing her friend was missing.

"Here!" she said bounding onto the stage with Pie, Suvi and Pinca.

"This one," said Felicity, as she took the microphone centre-stage, "is for friends forever!"

Put your heart
into practice

and you'll achieve
your perfect dream

Also available in the Felicity Wishes range:

Felicity Wishes: Secrets and Surprises

Felicity Wishes is planning her birthday party but it seems none of her friends can come. Will Felicity end up celebrating her birthday alone?

Felicity Wishes: Snowflakes and Sparkledust

It is time for spring to arrive in Little Blossoming but there is a problem and winter is staying put. Can Felicity Wishes get the seasons back on track?

If you enjoyed this book, why not
try another of these fantastic
story collections?

Clutter Clean-out

Designer Drama

Newspaper Nerves

Star Surprise

Enchanted Escape

Friends Forever

Sensational Secrets

Whispering Wishes